Grammy Loves You!

by Sally Helmick North

This book is a special reminder...

Grammy loves you!

Grammy sure loves you,
that's so true...

more than a fishie,
pink and blue.

More than a zebra,
with a polka-dot coat...

or a little pirate ducky,
on a teeny, tiny boat!

More than a penguin, singing a song...

or a cute little fly,
   who is buzzing right along!

More than a king crab,
laying in the sun...

or a bullfrog waiter,
serving everyone!

Grammy really loves you,
that you'll see...

more than a doggie,
happy as can be!

More than a hippo,
wearing a hat...

or a red and black tie
on a big, fat cat!

More than a starfish,
jumping in the sand...

or a crazy alligator,
in a rock and roll band!

More than a bunny,
with a Superman suit...

or a really tall giraffe!

That would surely be a hoot!

When the stars shine bright...

or the sky is blue...

Grammy really, really loves you...

That is TRUE! TRUE! TRUE!

Sally was born in Jackson, Michigan. She has lived all over the country with her husband, Fred.
They have 3 grown children, and they all live in Louisville, KY. She has written over 30 children's
books and had her first book published in 2000. Sneaky Snail Stories are all sweet and simple
rhyming books with really cute illustrations. You can see all the Sneaky Snail Stories at: www.
sneakysnailstories.com
Other books by Sally:

No Pancakes for Puppy
Grandma and Grandpa Love You
Your Aunt Loves You
The Best Day

Emma's Hilarious Horse Book (personalized for boys or girls with cats, dogs, penguins or frogs)
Emma, the Super, Amazing, Awesome, Intelligent, Girly-Girl (personalized)
Noah the Basketball Star (personalized for several sports for boys or girls)
Noah's Very Own Cook Book (personalized for boys or girls)
Grandma and Grandpa Love Emma (personalized from any relative for boys or girls)
Emma Turns One! (personalized for boys or girls ages 1-6)   and many more....

website: www.sneakysnailstories.com   facebook: Sneaky Snail Stories
Etsy: (search for) thesneakysnailstore   Amazon: (search for) Sally Helmick North

See all the Sneaky Snail Stories at: www.sneakysnailstories.com

The Best Day!

written and illustrated by Sally Helmick North

No Pancakes for Puppy!
written and illustrated by Sally Helmick North

No Cookies for Kitty!
written and illustrated by Sally Helmick North

Grandma and Grandpa Love You!

written and illustrated by Sally Helmick North

Made in the USA
Middletown, DE
14 February 2021

33702272R00015